WITHDRAWN

USBORNE

GREEK MYTHS
for young children

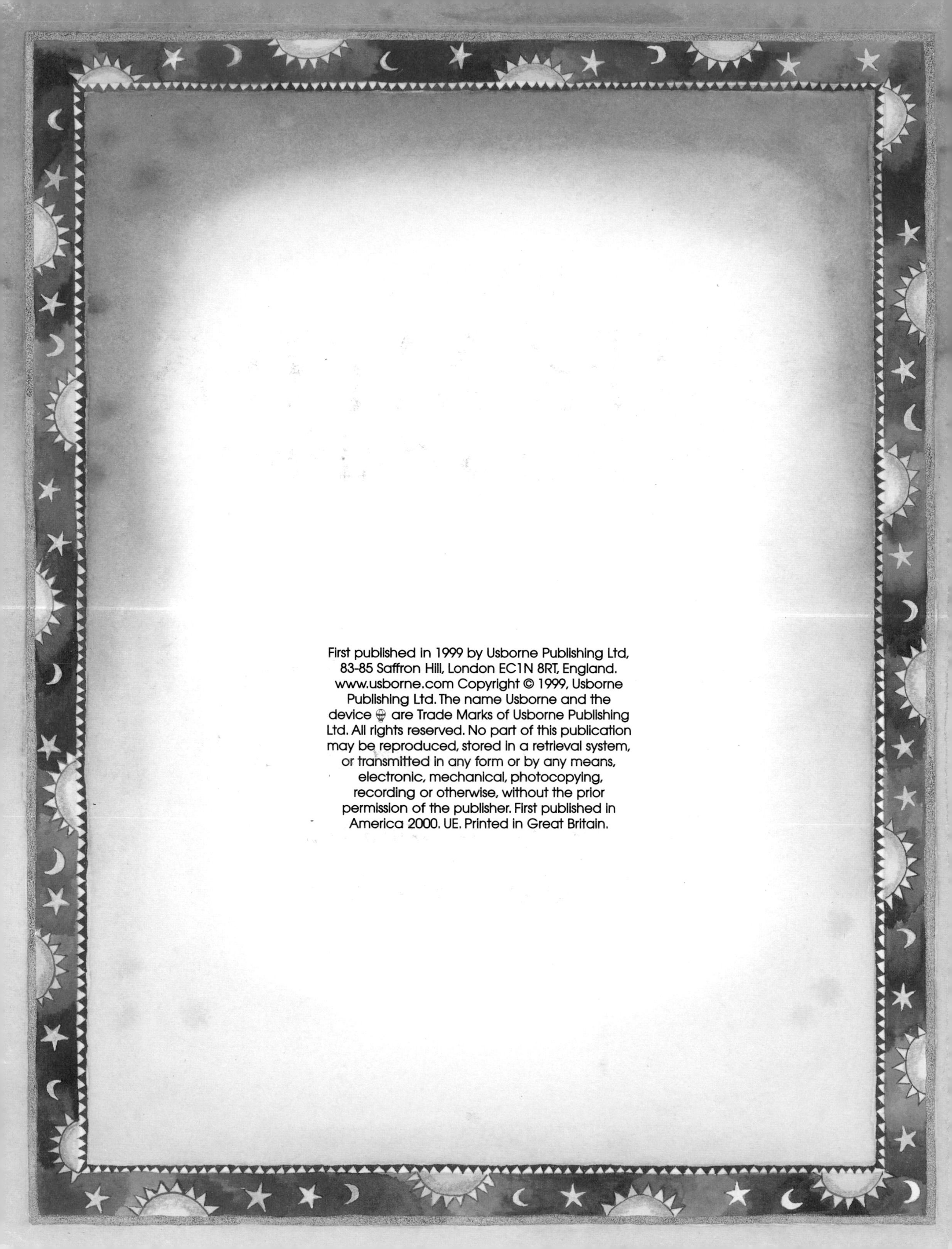

First published in 1999 by Usborne Publishing Ltd,
83-85 Saffron Hill, London EC1N 8RT, England.
www.usborne.com First published in
America 2000. UE. Printed in Great Britain.

USBORNE

GREEK MYTHS for young children

Retold by Heather Amery

Illustrated by Linda Edwards

Designed by Amanda Barlow

Edited by Jenny Tyler

Contents

About the Greek Myths

The Greeks, who lived thousands of years ago, had wonderful stories to tell about gods, monsters and brave heroes. They believed the gods and goddesses lived all around them, in the fields and woods, in the sea, under the ground and in great palaces among the towering peaks of Mount Olympus.

Sometimes the Greeks could see the gods and goddesses; sometimes they were invisible. They could be kind and helpful to the people they liked, but they could also be mean and spiteful, playing nasty tricks and appearing when least expected.

In the magical world of the Greek myths, ordinary mortals are caught up in extraordinary events, foolish and wicked people are punished, but the brave and daring are richly rewarded. Read on and enjoy these fascinating ancient stories which have stood the test of time.

The Gift of Fire

Long, long ago and far away the Greek gods and goddesses lived in palaces among the towering peaks of the great Mount Olympus. Zeus, the ruler of the gods, was wise and very powerful, but he could sometimes be spiteful and do foolish things. When he was angry, he fired thunderbolts from his fingers and all the other gods were a little scared of him. He married the goddess Hera and they had many children.

At first, the gods and goddesses ruled over an almost empty world; there were lots of animals roaming around but no people. The animals had been created by the god Epimetheus, who was very good at making things.

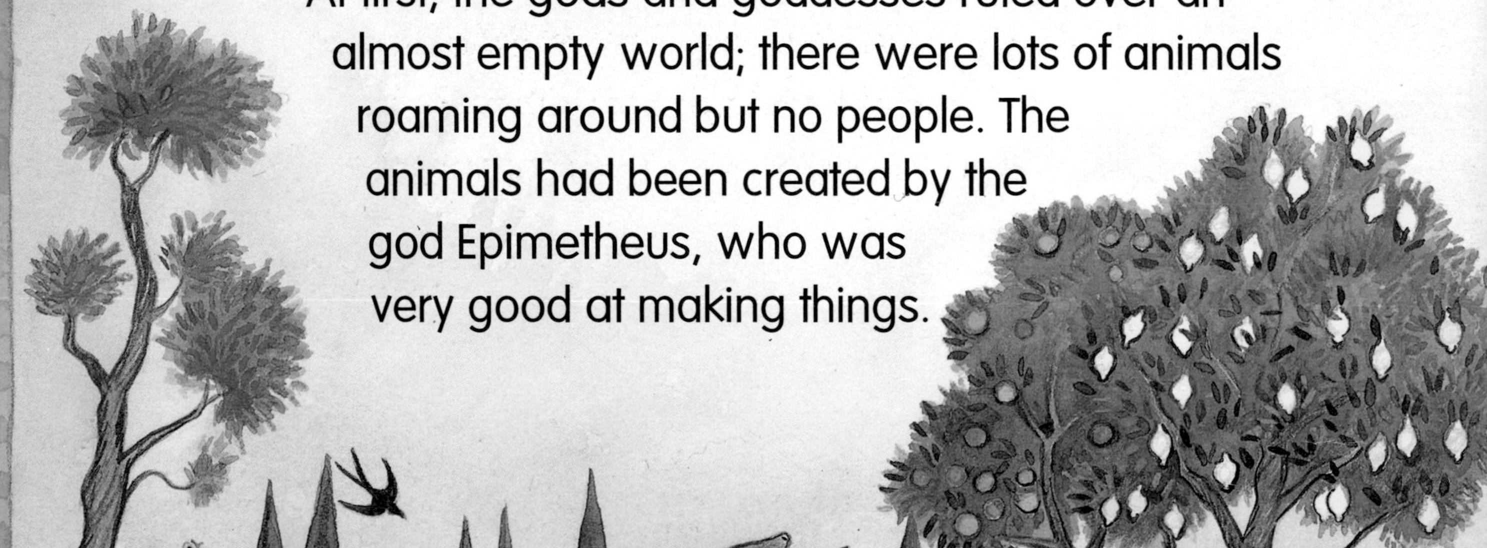

One day, Zeus
asked Prometheus, who was
Epimetheus's brother, to make
human beings to live in the world.

Prometheus picked up some mud. He shaped
lumps of it into men and women, making them
look just like the gods, and breathed on
them to make them come alive.

The people were happy on the Earth
but the one thing that Zeus wouldn't let
them have was fire. Prometheus loved
the people and felt sorry that they
had to shiver with cold through

the dark nights,
and eat raw food.

He went to Mount Olympus and, when no one was watching, stole a lump of burning charcoal from Zeus's palace. He took it to the people and showed them how to make fire with it. Now they could eat cooked food, and have warmth and light in the night. They were always very grateful to Prometheus and never forgot his special gift.

When Zeus noticed the smell of cooking and saw the fires glowing at night, he knew what Prometheus had done. He flew into a terrible rage. "Prometheus, how dare you go against my orders?" he shouted in a voice like thunder. "I'll punish you for this."

Zeus chained Prometheus to the side of a huge mountain. Every day an eagle flew down and tore out his liver, and every night it grew again. Prometheus was in terrible pain, but he couldn't die because he was a god. He had to stay there for hundreds of years until, at last, Zeus forgave him and he was rescued.

Pandora's Box

Zeus was very angry with the people who were so pleased with the gift of fire from Prometheus. He decided to punish them.

He asked the other gods to help him make a special woman. When they had finished, she was very beautiful; she was bright and clever, and could play lovely music. Zeus called her Pandora.

Then Zeus sent for Epimetheus. "Here is a wife for you, Epimetheus," he said. "She is a reward for making all the animals on the Earth." Zeus gave Pandora and Epimetheus a box which was bound and locked. "Take this box and keep it safe. I must warn you," said Zeus, "that you must never open it."

Epimetheus thanked Zeus and gazed at Pandora. She was so beautiful that he forgot that his brother, Prometheus, had warned him never to accept gifts from the other

gods. He took Pandora away and soon they were married. He put the box in a dark corner of his house.

Pandora was very happy with her new husband. The world was a wonderful place to live in. No one was ever ill or grew old.

No one was ever unkind or unpleasant. But Pandora was curious about the locked box and the more she thought about it, the more she wanted to know what was in it. Could it be jewels or some other precious things?

"Let's just have a little peek inside," she said to Epimetheus, smiling sweetly at him. "No, Zeus warned us never to open it," answered Epimetheus, frowning. He wanted to do everything he could to please his wife but he was scared of Zeus. Day after day Pandora begged Epimetheus to open the box and every day he refused.

One morning, when Epimetheus had gone out, Pandora crept into the room and stared at the box for a while. Then she made up her mind. She would open it.

She broke off the lock with a tool. Then, hardly daring to breathe, she slowly lifted the lid. Before she could look inside, there was a terrible screaming, wailing noise. She jumped back, terrified. Out of the box streamed all sorts of horrible things. There was hate and jealousy, cruelty and anger, hunger and poverty, pain and sickness, old age and death.

Pandora tried to slam down the lid but it was too late. Then one last thing, very small and pretty, fluttered out of the box. It was hope.

People would now suffer all kinds of terrible things, but because they had hope, they would never despair.

Persephone and the Seasons

One bright, sunny morning, the goddess Demeter said goodbye to her daughter Persephone. "I'll be back for supper," she called. Demeter was the goddess of all the plants in the world. She made sure the corn grew tall in the fields and fruit ripened on the trees. The weather was always fine and there were harvests all the year.

After her mother had gone, Persephone went out to meet her friends and pick flowers with them. Searching for the very best lilies, she wandered away and was soon on her own.

Suddenly, she heard a noise and looked up. She saw a chariot pulled by four black horses, driven by Pluto,

god of the Underworld. Pluto had fallen in love with Persephone, but knew Demeter would never allow him to marry her daughter.

Before Persephone could scream, Pluto dragged her into the chariot and raced away. As they thundered across the ground, a huge cleft opened. Pluto drove straight down it and the ground closed up behind them. He and Persephone had disappeared into the Underworld.

When Demeter came back that evening, she called to Persephone but there was no reply. The house was empty. When it grew dark, Demeter began to worry. Where could Persephone be? At midnight, she lit a flaming torch and set out to look for her. All night she searched, calling, "Persephone, Persephone, where are you?" But there was no answer. For nine days and nine nights, Demeter searched, not stopping to sleep or even to eat.

Dressed in black instead of her usual bright clothes, Demeter wandered all over the country as a haggard, old woman. Because she no longer looked after the crops, the corn rotted in the fields, no fruit ripened on the trees and the grass turned brown. There was nothing for the sheep and goats to eat and all the people grew short of food. Soon they were near to starving.

Zeus called a meeting of all the gods and goddesses. "This is very serious," he said in the voice that rolled like thunder. "Unless we can persuade Demeter to take care of the Earth again, all the people will die."

"Pluto must let Persephone leave the Underworld," said a goddess. "Only then will Demeter save the Earth."

Zeus called for Hermes, the messenger of the gods. "Go to Pluto and ask him, very politely, to return Persephone to her mother," he said. Hermes flew off at once. Only the gods and goddesses could go into the Underworld, the home of all the people who had died, and come out again.

"I will never let Persephone go," growled Pluto. "I love her and I want to marry her." "Please, Pluto," begged Hermes, "please be reasonable. You know Persephone doesn't love you and won't marry you."

"Very well," roared Pluto, very angry. "I'll let her go if she hasn't eaten any food while she's been here. You know the rule. If she has eaten anything in the Underworld, she must stay here forever."

"That's easy," said Hermes. "Let's ask her." Persephone cried, in answer to the question, "I couldn't eat anything here. I've never touched even the smallest crumb of food."

A misty ghost of a gardener was listening. "Oh yes you did," he croaked. "I saw you. You picked a ripe pomegranate and ate it."

"No, no," cried Persephone, "I didn't eat it all. I was so thirsty, I just swallowed a few of the seeds." "That's enough," shouted Pluto.

"Please, Pluto," begged Hermes, "let her go for a little while. A few seeds aren't much." "Oh, all right," growled Pluto. "Persephone may go back to the Earth for half of each year but must spend the other months here with me, in the Underworld."

Holding Persephone's hand, Hermes flew with her out of the Underworld to Demeter. "Oh, my darling daughter," cried Demeter, hugging Persephone. "You have come back to me at last." "Yes," sobbed Persephone, "but I must go back to the Underworld for part of every year."

Demeter knew she had to accept this. At once, she looked young again. She put on her brightest clothes and began work, making new shoots of corn and grass grow and leaves open on the trees. It was spring all over the Earth.

All through the summer Demeter was happy and busy, watching the fine harvests of corn and fruit. But when Persephone had to go back to the Underworld, she was sad and it became autumn. The leaves on the trees turned brown, the grass stopped growing and the weather turned cold. It was winter, until Persephone returned. Then Demeter was happy and it was spring again.

The Story of Arachne

Arachne sat at her loom, weaving brilliant threads into wonderful patterns. She smiled as she worked and sang a happy little song. People in her village and from all over the country came to see the beautiful things this young girl wove. Arachne loved hearing them tell her how clever she was and she grew very conceited.

"I can weave better patterns than even the goddess Athene," she boasted to an old woman.

"Hush, Athene may hear you," whispered the woman.

"I don't care," said Arachne loudly.

Now, everyone knew that it was very dangerous to talk about the gods and goddesses. If they heard something they didn't like, they could play nasty tricks on people.

At that moment, Athene appeared in the doorway of Arachne's house. Arachne leapt up from her loom and knelt in front of the goddess of weaving, looking proudly up at her.

"I think I heard you speak my name," said Athene. "I've come to see your weaving." She smiled but her voice was so icy, everyone watching scurried away in fright. Athene looked at the weaving on the loom. "Yes," she said, "I have to admit it is very good."

"Could you do better?" asked Arachne, boldly.

"We shall see," answered Athene. "We will have a competition, you and I, and then we shall see."

Athene and Arachne set to work at their looms, weaving away for days. They used the brightest threads and most unusual patterns. At last, the two pieces were finished. They took them off the looms and laid them down, side by side. Everyone came to admire them and try to decide which was best.

Athene stared at the two lovely pieces of weaving in silence. Then she screamed with rage. Although she would never admit it, she could see that Arachne's weaving was better than her own. She grabbed it and ripped it from top to bottom.

"As you are so clever at weaving," she screamed at the terrified Arachne, "you shall weave forever, and no one will ever want what you weave."

She tapped Arachne lightly on her shoulder. The girl dropped to the ground. As everyone watched in horror, she shrivelled to a small dark blob, grew eight legs and ran away into a dark corner. Athene had turned Arachne into a spider. From that moment on, Arachne and all her many descendants have woven beautiful webs. You may see them in dusty corners or sparkling with dew in the early morning.

The Many Tasks of Heracles

The great god Zeus had a son, called Heracles. The other gods and goddesses gave the boy wonderful gifts, making him immensely strong and very brave, but also kind and gentle. Hera, Zeus's wife, hated her baby step-son. One day, she sent two deadly snakes slithering into his cradle. Although he was only a few months old, Heracles strangled them both and tossed them aside, laughing and gurgling. Hera then hated him even more.

When Heracles grew up, he was taught to use a bow and arrow, wrestle, and play the lute. He married Megara, the daughter of King Creon, and had many children. He was soon famous for his brave deeds and great strength. But Hera was watching him, furious that he was so happy and successful. One day, she made him go crazy and, in a terrible rage, he killed all his children.

When he was sane again, Heracles was horrified at what he'd done.

He at once went to the temple of the gods and begged to be told what he had to do to be forgiven. "Go to King Eurystheus at Tiryns," said a priestess, "and work for him as a slave, doing whatever tasks he gives you."

The Man-Eating Lion

King Eurystheus gave Heracles the worst tasks he could think of. "First," he ordered, "you must kill the huge lion that has been terrorizing my people."

Heracles went off at once to search for the lion. It took him weeks to find a trail of its huge paw prints.

He followed them to a cave, then hid and waited for the lion to come out. When it was close enough, Heracles hurled his spear but it just bounced off the lion. Then he tried to slash it with his sword, but it left no mark at all. In despair, he hit it as hard as he could with his club. The lion was stunned for a moment, then slunk back to its cave. Heracles ran after it and grabbed it. He fought the lion for hours in the dark until, at last, he strangled it.

He dragged the dead lion from the cave and carried it all the way back to King Eurystheus's palace to prove he'd killed the beast. The King was so frightened, he jumped into a huge brass pot. "Never bring your trophies into my palace again," he shouted.

Heracles made a cloak out of the lion's skin. Nothing could pierce it and he wore it for protection. It saved his life many times.

The Nine-Headed Hydra

"Your next task, slave," King Eurystheus said to Heracles, "is to kill the Hydra which lives in the Argos marshes." Heracles rode to the stinking swamps with his nephew, Iolaus. He fired burning arrows into the Hydra's lair to drive it out. When it crawled out, they saw it had a body like a dog and nine heads like snakes. These spat deadly poison. Heracles ran up to it and chopped off one of its heads, but immediately a new one grew in its place.

Heracles realized he couldn't overcome this monster on his own. He called to Iolaus for help. "Set fire to a branch and bring it to me," he shouted.

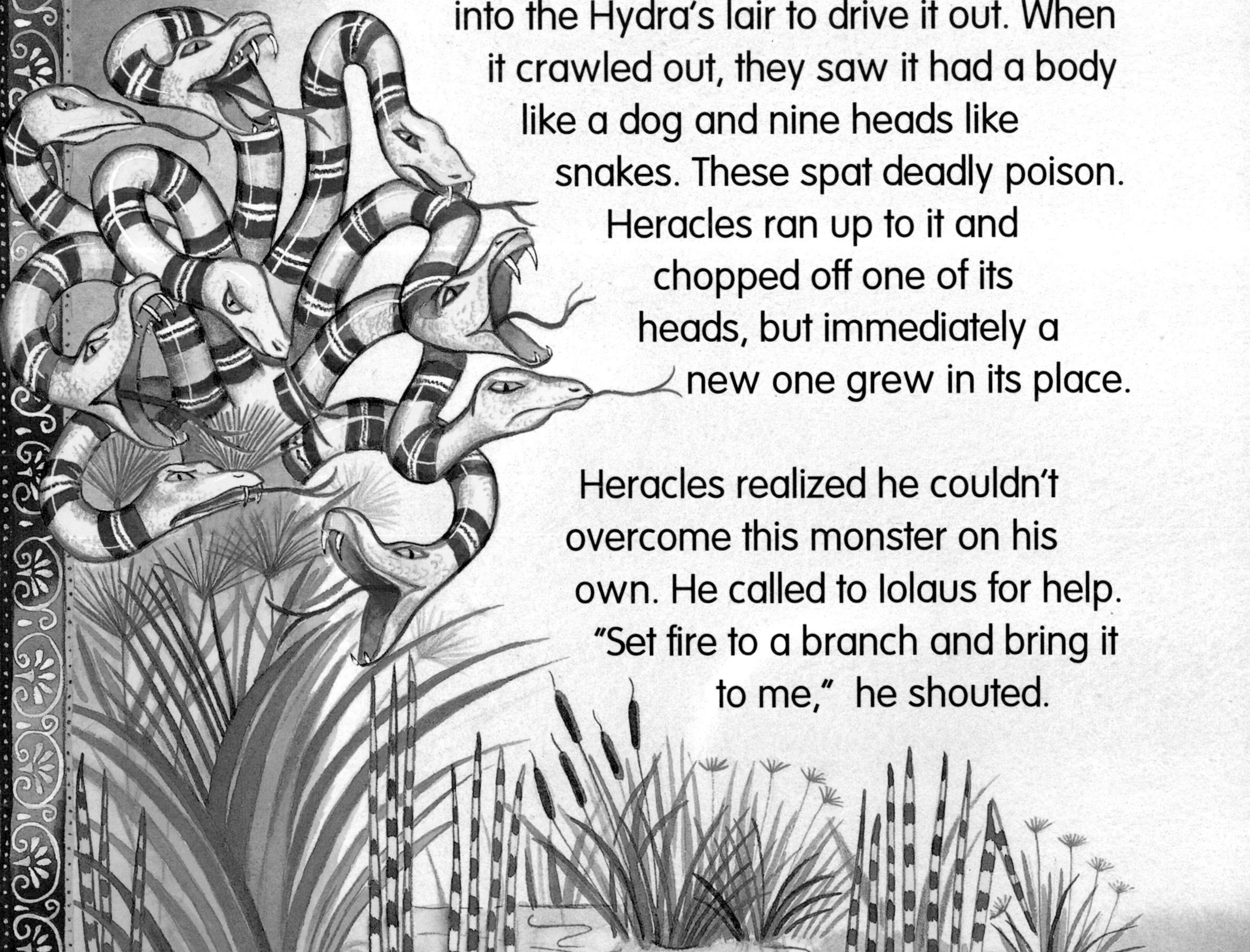

Holding his breath to avoid the poison, Heracles ran back to the Hydra. First he chopped off a head, then he burned the neck with fire from the branch so it couldn't grow again. When he had cut off all the heads, the monster was dead.

Heracles dipped the tips of his arrows in its blood, which was a deadly poison. "These may be useful one day," he said to Iolaus, and they rode back to King Eurystheus for Heracles's third task.

The Stag with Golden Antlers

"You must bring me the stag with golden antlers, but you must not hurt it in any way," commanded King Eurystheus. Heracles set out at once and chased the stag through woods and forests for a whole year. It was the most beautiful and fastest of all the deer, and Heracles could never quite catch up with it.

At last, he saw it standing still on a river bank. He crept through the bushes without making a sound. The stag put down its head to drink the water and didn't see Heracles. Silently he ran up to it and flung a net over it. It struggled but couldn't escape. Heracles gently tied the stag's legs together, lifted it up on his massive shoulders and began the long journey back to the King.

"Stop!" Heracles was startled by an angry shout. The goddess Artemis appeared in front of him. "What are you doing with my stag?" she demanded. "I'm taking it to King Eurystheus," replied Heracles, and explained about his tasks.

"You may go on, but you must promise to return the stag, unharmed, to the forest," ordered Artemis. Heracles thanked her and promised to do as she said. He trudged on to the palace and showed the stag to King Eurystheus. Then he released it safely in the woods.

The Huge Wild Boar

The King tried hard to think of an even more difficult task for Heracles. "There's a wild boar in Arcadia which is so savage, it is destroying all the farms and villages," he said. "Go and capture it and bring it back here, alive."

Heracles set out the next day. On the way, he met a centaur, which had the body of a horse and the head of a man. The centaur invited him to stop for a meal. Heracles readily agreed and soon the two were feasting merrily. But other centaurs smelled the food and wine and were furious that they hadn't been invited. They attacked, trying to steal the feast. Heracles grabbed his bow and drove them away with a shower of arrows.

Next morning, Heracles continued his search and, after five days, he found the tracks of an immense boar in the snow on a mountain. He followed them until he saw the boar itself, moving clumsily through the snow. He watched it, thinking up a plan.

Hiding behind a rock, Heracles shouted as loudly as he could. Startled, the boar blundered away into a deep snowdrift and was trapped. Heracles leapt out of his hiding place, grabbed the boar and tied it up in chains. Heaving the great beast on his back, he wearily carried it back to the palace. The minute the King saw the boar he was so frightened, he jumped back into his brass pot again.

The Augean Stables

When Eurystheus had overcome his fright, he summoned Heracles. He was angry that Heracles had completed the last task so quickly, and tried to think of something that was really impossible.

"Go to King Augeas and clean his stables. Do it in one day," he ordered. King Augeas laughed when Heracles told him what he had come to do. "Those stables haven't been cleaned for years and years," he said. "But you're welcome to try. I'd like them cleaned out," he added, and laughed again.

Very early next morning, Heracles went to the stables and looked at the heaps of stinking horse manure. He couldn't carry it away; it would take years, and he had only one day.

Then he had an idea. Not far away was a river. All day he worked, building a dam and digging a channel from the river to the stables. When everything was ready, he broke the dam and sent the river roaring straight to the stables. The torrent of water gushed through one end of the building and out through the other end, washing out all the dirt and carrying it away to the sea.

In one day, Heracles had cleaned the stables, leaving them shining and sweet-smelling. By the evening he had changed the river back to its proper course. King Augeas was absolutely delighted when he saw what Heracles had done, and said it was a clever trick.

When Heracles returned to the palace, King Eurystheus was *not* delighted. He also thought it was a trick and that Heracles had cheated; cleaning the stables like that didn't count as a task. He went away to think of something even more difficult for Heracles to do.

The Stymphalian Birds

"These birds live in Arcadia and they eat people," said King Eurystheus. "They have brass wings, beaks and claws. You must get rid of them."

Heracles began the long journey to Arcadia. At last, he came to a muddy lake with an island in the middle. This is where the birds lived. Heracles tried to wade through the mud to the island but sank in so deeply, he had to return to dry land. Then he found a boat, hidden in the reeds. He tried to row it to the island but that, too, became stuck in the mud and he had to wade back.

He couldn't think how he could get to the island, so he

prayed to the goddess
Athene. She appeared at once, holding
a brass rattle. "Take this," she said, "and
shake it at the birds." Heracles just had time to
thank her before she disappeared.

He climbed a mountain overlooking the lake and shook
the rattle as hard as he could. It made such a terrible
noise, the birds on the island flew up into the air,
screaming and whistling. Heracles shot many of them
with his poisoned arrows, and the others flew away.
He waited until sunset but they didn't come back.

He carefully picked up two dead birds to show to King
Eurystheus. "They don't look very dangerous
to me," grumbled the King. Heracles glared
angrily at him but said nothing.

The Great Bull of Crete

King Eurystheus thought the next task he gave to Heracles would take him away for a long time. "Go to the island of Crete," he ordered. "There is a huge, white, fire-breathing bull. It is running wild, destroying the farms and killing the people. You must capture it and bring it back here, alive."

Heracles strode down to the port and found a ship and a crew willing to sail to Crete. The sea voyage was a long one but, at last, they saw the tall cliffs of the island. Once ashore, Heracles was met by King Minos. "You are welcome here," said the King, and invited Heracles to his palace. Heracles explained why he had come and the King was very pleased that he would be rid of the terrible beast. "But be warned," he said. "It's no ordinary bull."

Next morning, Heracles began his search. He found the bull quite close to the city. He hid among some olive trees and watched it for a few minutes. He had never seen a bull that was so enormous or so fierce. Then he stepped out into the open.

The bull looked up, saw Heracles and pawed the ground, snorting fire from its nostrils. Then it charged. Heracles wrapped his lion skin around him and waited until the bull was almost on him. Then he quickly stepped aside. As the great beast thundered past, Heracles grabbed one of its horns and swung himself on to its back.

The bull tried to toss him off but Heracles clung on. It pranced and snorted, raced around and bucked, but it couldn't throw Heracles off its back. Growing tired at last, it came to a trembling standstill. Heracles jumped down, dragged it back to his ship and sailed away.

King Eurystheus was so frightened when he saw the bull, he jumped into his brass pot again.

The Man-Eating Horses

When King Eurystheus climbed out of his pot, he said to Heracles, "Your next task is to go to King Diomedes and bring back his four wild horses. They're not very nice. They eat people."

This time, Heracles took four brave friends with him. When they arrived at Diomedes's palace, the King pretended he was very pleased to see them, but Heracles was suspicious. He didn't trust King Diomedes.

After a grand feast that evening, Heracles and his friends went to bed. "Don't go to sleep. I think the King plans to kill us," Heracles whispered. "I've heard he feeds his guests to his horses." No one came near them in the night and, just before dawn, Heracles and his friends climbed out of their bedroom windows and crept silently to the stables.

They knocked out the sleepy guards and broke open the stable doors. The horses, which were chained to a wood beam, stamped and snorted at the strangers. Heracles chopped down the beam to free them. "Hurry back to the ship," he shouted, and they drove the horses down to the beach.

Before they reached the ship, they saw King Diomedes and his soldiers racing straight for them. "You hold the horses," Heracles shouted to one of his friends. "The rest of you get ready to fight."

The battle was short but very fierce. When it was over, King Diomedes and his men lay dead. Heracles ran back to the horses, only to find they had eaten his friend. In a furious rage, he fed the King to them. The horses then became calm and very docile. He led them to the ship and sailed back to King Eurystheus.

King Eurystheus was terrified of the horses. "Take the horrid things away," he screamed. Heracles led them out of the palace and set them free in the mountains.

The Amazon Queen's Belt

"My daughter," King Eurystheus said to Heracles, "wants the belt Queen Hippolyta always wears around her waist. Go and get it for her."

When Heracles's friends heard he was going to the Amazons, they all wanted to go with him. The Amazons were a race of fierce women warriors who lived on the Black Sea. Everyone had heard stories about them but no one had ever seen them.

Heracles chose a band of the bravest men and they boarded a ship one morning, setting sail for a long voyage. At last they saw land. "Arm yourselves, men," shouted Heracles, "and be ready to fight."

When the ship reached the shore, Heracles and his men were surprised to see a group of women walking along the sand, smiling and waving. "You are very welcome here," cried the leader. "I am Queen Hippolyta. Come to my palace for food and wine." Heracles and his men were delighted not to have to fight a battle.

At the palace, Heracles told Hippolyta why he had come. "You may have my belt as a present," she said, smiling at him. The goddess Hera was watching, and was furious that this task was to be so easy for Heracles. She whispered in the other women's ears, "Beware, Heracles has come to harm Queen Hippolyta."

The Amazon women believed her and, snatching up their

swords and spears, they attacked Heracles. His men fought bravely and, in the thick of the battle, Heracles killed Hippolyta.

"Run back to the ship," he shouted to his men and, grabbing Hippolyta's belt, Heracles raced to the beach. The Amazon women chased them but they managed to sail away safely. Heracles had the precious belt, but he was very sad that he had killed Hippolyta for it.

Eurystheus's daughter was delighted with the belt, but the King growled at Heracles, "You have more tasks to do."

The Cattle of Geryon

"Go to King Geryon, the three-headed ogre, and bring his cattle back here," ordered King Eurystheus. Next day, Heracles sailed across from Greece to North Africa. Trudging along the coast, he grew so hot, he angrily fired an arrow at Helios, the god of the sun. Helios was amused by such boldness, and cooled down the sun's rays. When Heracles reached the place where he had to cross the sea, Helios sent down a huge golden bowl that floated on the water. Heracles climbed in the strange boat and drifted across to Geryon's kingdom.

He pulled the golden boat up the beach and went in search of the cattle. Soon he saw them high up on a hill. As he climbed up to them, a huge dog with two heads leapt out at him, snarling and growling. Heracles waited until it was close, raised his club and killed it with one mighty blow.

He was driving the cattle down the hill when King Geryon came rushing after him, shouting angrily. Heracles fitted an arrow into his bow and shot Geryon, killing him instantly. Heracles drove the cattle down to his golden bowl boat, loaded them on board and sailed away.

When, many weeks later, Heracles drove King Geryon's cattle into the palace yard, King Eurystheus took no notice of the cattle and just complained that Heracles had been away far too long.

The Golden Apples

"You must now bring me three golden apples from the Tree of Hesperides," King Eurystheus commanded Heracles. Heracles had no idea where the Tree was and begged the goddess Athene to help him.

"You'll find it in a sacred grove in the mountains at the end of the Earth," said Athene. Heracles thanked her and, after many months, he reached the Earth's end and saw Atlas, who held up the sky. "How can I get the golden apples?" Heracles asked Atlas. "Go to the Tree and kill the dragon which guards them. Then come back here. Only I can pick the apples," said Atlas, groaning under the weight of the sky.

Heracles thanked him and crept into the sacred grove to the Tree. Coiled around its trunk was a golden dragon with golden eyes. It glared at Heracles, daring him to come near. Heracles shot it with a poisoned arrow. Then he went back to Atlas.

"Hold the sky for me, while I go and pick the apples," said Atlas. Heracles did as Atlas said, and Atlas went away and came back with three golden apples. "Hang onto the sky a bit longer and I'll take them to King Eurystheus for you," said Atlas. Heracles suspected a trick; he thought Atlas would never return and he'd have to hold up the sky forever.

"Thank you," said Heracles, "but, before you go, could you just help me to make the weight more comfortable. Take it for a moment while I settle my cloak on my shoulders." And he passed the sky to Atlas. When he was free, Heracles picked up the three golden apples, said goodbye to Atlas, and hurried back to King Eurystheus.

Guard Dog of the Underworld

"Your last task is the most difficult of all," King Eurystheus said to Heracles. "Go to the Underworld and bring back Cerebus, the fierce three-headed dog which guards its gates."

Heracles knew he couldn't find his way to the Underworld on his own. He again asked the goddess Athene for help and she sent Hermes, the gods' messenger, to guide him. Together, they walked through tunnels to the black River Styx which you had to cross to get into the Underworld.

There Charon, an old boatman, refused to take them across. "You know I can only take dead people," he said grumpily. Heracles argued with him for so long that Charon agreed to ferry him across, but not Hermes.

On the other side of the river, Heracles walked through more misty tunnels, past drifting ghosts of the dead. At last, he saw Pluto, the King of the Underworld, and Persephone, sitting on their misty thrones. "Please may I take Cerebus away with me?" he asked.

"You may take the dog, but you must return it unharmed," said Pluto. Heracles thanked Pluto and hurried to the Underworld's gates where Cerebus stood guard. The dog's three heads barked and growled at him.

Heracles crouched, waiting. When Cerebus leapt at him, he wrestled with the dog until it lay still, exhausted.

Then he dragged the dog back to the River Styx, into the boat, and then all the way back to King Eurystheus's palace.

When the King saw the dog, growling and snarling, he screamed with fright and jumped into his pot again. "There," shouted Heracles, "I've completed my tasks. I'm no longer your slave. I am free," and he dragged Cerebus back to the Underworld.

Then he went to the temple of the gods and knelt in front of the priestess. "Heracles," she said, "you have proved you are strong and very brave. You are forgiven for killing your children."

Heracles thanked her and quietly left the temple. The gods and goddesses were so pleased with Heracles, they invited him to Mount Olympus. Zeus, his father, greeted him. "You have done well," he thundered. Heracles stayed in his palace for a while before leaving for many more adventures.

Echo and Narcissus

Echo was a wood nymph who could never stop talking. She strolled through the forests, always chattering away and giggling very loudly. The goddess Hera was irritated by the noise and asked her to be quiet, but Echo couldn't stop. When Hera found out that, as well as always prattling on and on, Echo also told her lies, she was very angry.

She pointed her finger at Echo and ordered, "Be silent. From now on, you will repeat only what other people say to you." Echo opened her mouth to protest but no words came. She couldn't speak.

"You may go now," commanded Hera. "Go now," repeated Echo. She tried to scream but couldn't make a sound. Horrified, she stumbled away through the woods, lonely and miserable. None of her friends wanted to be with her now.

One day she saw Narcissus. Echo hid and watched him. She had never seen such a handsome young man and she fell hopelessly in love with him. Every day she followed him, and he often caught sight of her. At first, he took no notice of her; he was very used to girls falling in love with him. Then he grew irritated that everywhere he went, Echo was there too.

"Go away. I don't love you," he shouted. "Love you, love you," repeated Echo. "Leave me alone," called Narcissus. "Alone, alone," replied Echo.

She wandered sadly away through the trees and, as the weeks passed, she grew thinner and paler until she faded away altogether; nothing of her was left except her voice, which always repeated what anyone said.

Narcissus didn't even notice that he no longer saw Echo in the woods, although sometimes he still heard her voice. The goddess Artemis decided to punish Narcissus for being so vain and cruel. When he was alone, she made him sit down by a pool and gaze into the dark water. There he saw the reflection of his face and, never having seen himself in a mirror, didn't know he was looking at himself. He had never seen such a beautiful face before and fell in love with it.

Day after day, he lay staring into the pool. He was puzzled that when he spoke the lips of the face moved too. When he tried to kiss the face and touched the water, it disappeared in the ripples. If he waited until the water grew still, he could see the face again. Many times he begged the face to come out and love him, but it never stirred.

Feeling rejected, Narcissus could bear it no longer and he killed himself. Where his body lay, a tall flower with white petals grew. You can see this pretty flower in the spring. It is called a narcissus.

Daedalus and Icarus

Minos, the King of Crete, was a very cruel, wicked man. One day, he sent a message to Daedalus, who was famous as a sculptor and inventor. "Come to my island, and bring your son with you," wrote King Minos. "I have work for you."

Daedalus and his son, Icarus, sailed at once for Crete and were greeted by the King in his huge palace at Knossos. "I want you to build a secret maze in the cellars of my palace," Minos ordered. "You are to tell no one about it. It must have so many winding tunnels that anyone going into it will never be able to come out again. I shall call it the Labyrinth."

Daedalus didn't know why the King wanted this strange cellar, but he and Icarus did as the King commanded and set to work. When the Labyrinth was finally finished, Daedalus discovered its secret. It was to be a prison where Minos could keep a terrible monster, called the Minotaur, which had the head of a bull and the body of a man. It ate people.

When Daedalus went to the King to ask for payment for his work, Minos refused. "You and your son are the only people in the world who know how to go into the Labyrinth and come out alive," he shouted. "I cannot let you go."

The King called his guards, and Daedalus and Icarus were marched away. They were locked up in a tall tower. Although they were well fed, they longed to escape. Daedalus watched the birds flying over the island and out to sea. Then he had an idea.

Every day he put out food for the birds which came to the window and every day he collected some of their feathers. After many months, he set to work secretly so the guards never saw what he was doing.

One morning, Daedalus woke Icarus very early. "Everything is ready," he whispered. "We are leaving." Icarus stared as his father pulled out from under his bed four huge wings he had made from feathers held together with wax.

"Stand up," Daedalus said to Icarus, "and I'll fasten two

wings to your shoulders and arms." Then he told Icarus how to attach the other wings to his shoulders. "We're ready now," he said. "Come to the window."

Together they stood on the window ledge. Icarus looked down. "I'm scared," he said, his voice shaking. "Will the wings really work?" "Just follow me," said Daedalus, "and do what I do. Don't fly too low over the sea or the spray will wet the feathers. And don't fly too high or the sun will melt the wax on the wings."

"Here I go," shouted Daedalus, and leapt off the window ledge. Icarus watched him glide down, holding out his wings. Then, taking a deep breath, Icarus jumped. At first he dropped down, but soon felt his open wings holding him up in the air. He glided gently after Daedalus.

"This is wonderful," he shouted. "We really are flying."

They flew away over the island. They had escaped from their prison tower. Very excited, Icarus swooped down over the sea, and then soared up high in the sky. He'd forgotten what Daedalus said about not going near the sun and, as he glided around and around, the heat melted the wax and the feathers began to fall off the wings.

As Daedalus watched in horror, Icarus plummeted like a stone down into the sea, and drowned. There was nothing he could do to save his son. Very sadly, he flew on and landed safely in Sicily.

Bellerophon and the Flying Horse

Prince Bellerophon was exiled from his own country, but lived happily in the court of King Proteus. All went well until the King's wife told her husband that the young, handsome prince had insulted her. The King didn't know that this wasn't true and was very, very angry. He wanted to kill Bellerophon, but he felt he couldn't do harm to a guest without offending the gods, and that could have terrible consequences.

To get rid of Bellerophon, the King said to him, "Please take this letter to Iobates, the King of Lycia." Bellerophon willingly took the letter, not knowing that it asked King Iobates to kill him.

When Bellerophon arrived safely at Iobates's court after a long and dangerous journey, Iobates welcomed him. He put the letter from King Proteus aside and forgot to open it for nine days. By that time, he had grown to like the good-natured prince and he, too, felt he couldn't kill a guest.

Then King Iobates thought of the Chimaera. This monster had a head like a lion, a body like a goat and a snake for a tail. "I need a brave man like you," King Iobates said to Bellerophon. "Please go and rid my kingdom of this terrible creature. It's killing my people and ruining their land. Lots of men have tried to fight it, and have died bravely. I'm sure you could kill it," he added, although he was quite certain the Chimaera would kill Bellerophon first.

The young prince accepted the challenge. Before he set out, a wise old man said to him, "You won't be able to kill that monster unless you are riding on Pegasus, the horse with huge white wings. No one has ever ridden him yet."

Bellerophon didn't know if he should believe the old man and set out to find the Chimaera. On the way, the goddess Athene suddenly appeared in front of him. "Take this," she said, and handed him a golden bridle. Before he could thank her, she vanished.

One evening, Bellerophon saw Pegasus, drinking at a stream. Creeping very quietly closer, he flung the bridle over the horse's head and clung on when the beautiful horse snorted, bucked and reared, trying to escape.

At last, it stood still and Bellerophon climbed on its back.

Pegasus flapped its wings and leapt into the air. Soon they were soaring over the land, across plains and mountains, until Bellerophon saw the Chimaera below him. He pulled on the bridle, and Pegasus swooped down.

Safe on Pegasus's back, Bellerophon dodged the fire which poured out of the monster's mouth and the snake tail which spat poison. He fired an arrow into its side,

and then one into its mouth, which killed it.
The Chimaera was dead.

Bellerophon returned to a hero's welcome. King Iobates was delighted to be rid of the Chimaera and said to the young prince. "You may marry my daughter, and have some good land to live on."

Over the next few years, Bellerophon grew famous for his brave deeds and was praised wherever he went, but he grew conceited and when people said he was like a god, he started to believe them.

Bellerophon thought if he was like a god, he should visit the gods. He leapt astride Pegasus and urged him to fly to Mount Olympus. Zeus, the ruler of the gods, was furious. He sent an insect to sting Pegasus under the tail, making the horse rear and fling Bellerophon off its back.

Zeus watched him fall to the ground. Bellerophon didn't die but he was wounded. Alone and unhappy, he roamed the land. No one would go near a man who had made Zeus so angry.

Jason and the Golden Fleece

Jason was only a baby when his wicked Uncle Pelias stole his father's kingdom. To keep him safe, Jason's father secretly sent his young son far away to the mountains. There he lived in a cave, looked after by Cheiron, a wise old centaur who was half man and half horse. Cheiron taught him to wrestle, shoot with bows and arrows, and many other things.

When Jason was twenty-one, Cheiron said to him, "It's time for you to go to your Uncle Pelias and demand the throne that is rightfully yours."

Jason set out for the city of Iolcus, where his Uncle lived. On the way, he had to cross a wide river. Sitting on the bank was an old woman. "Young man," she croaked, "will you help me across the river?" Jason looked at the old woman and then at the swirling water in dismay, but he had a kind heart. "Climb on my back," he said, and bending down, he helped her up.

He began to wade across the river but the water grew deeper and deeper, and the old woman on his back grew heavier and heavier. Just managing to keep his head above the water, Jason struggled on, but lost one of his sandals in the river mud.

Panting and tired, he reached the other bank and gently put the old woman down. "Continue your journey and, one day, you will be a great hero," she said. Just as Jason was going to ask her what she meant, she vanished. He didn't realize she was the goddess Hera.

After a rest, Jason walked on and, after many days, reached the city of Iolcus. When he walked through the streets, everyone stared at the young man with only one sandal. He strode on, straight to Pelias's palace. His uncle was terrified because he had been warned that, one day, a man with one sandal would come and take his throne.

"I know who you are and why you have come," Pelias said to Jason. "You may have the throne if you bring me the Golden Fleece from Colchis." Pelias was certain Jason would never succeed. He knew the journey was very long and very dangerous, and that the Golden Fleece was guarded by a fierce serpent that never, ever closed its golden eyes.

Jason had no fear, and immediately agreed to go and search for the Golden Fleece. He went to the seashore and asked Argus, a boat-builder, to build him a special ship. When it was finished, Jason called it The Argo. It was beautiful, long, fast and sleek, with oars, a stout mast and one huge sail.

As Jason stood looking at it, the goddess Athene suddenly appeared in front of him. She handed him an oak branch. "Take this. It will protect your ship." Jason was pleased and thanked her. Then he carefully fastened the magic oak branch to the front of The Argo.

The Argo Sets Sail

When news of Jason's voyage spread, princes, brave adventurers, the sons of gods and many others wanted to join the crew. Jason chose fifty of them. Among them was Orpheus who played the lyre and sang so sweetly that even wild animals came near to listen. Then there was Atalanta, the huntress, and mighty Heracles, and the twin sons of the North Wind who had golden wings on their ankles and could fly. Jason called his crew the Argonauts.

One morning at dawn, they loaded the ship with food and jars of fresh water, and set off.

Crowds on the shore watched them go and cheered as they rowed away. At first, the sea was rough, and strong winds blew against the ship. Then the gods decided to help and a good breeze came from the right direction. The crew hoisted the sail and the ship moved briskly over the water.

Over the next few weeks, the Argonauts had to pass through dangerous rocky waters and stormy seas. When they landed on islands for fresh food and water, they were often attacked by fierce people or bloodthirsty monsters. But they fought bravely and sailed safely on.

The Harpies

Nearing the entrance to the Black Sea, the Argonauts stopped at an island to ask King Phineus for his advice on the dangers to come. They found Phineus, who was very old and blind, in a dark, gloomy house. "I will help you," croaked the King, "if you will get rid of the Harpies for me. Every time I try to eat, they fly down and steal my food. I'm starving."

The Argonauts laid out a meal, and at once the Harpies came screaming out of the sky. They had the faces of hideous women and bodies like vultures. The men attacked them with their swords. Some Harpies escaped but the twin sons of the North Wind flew after them, chasing them across the sea so that they never returned.

The Clashing Rocks

While the Argonauts waited for the twins to come back, they prepared a great feast for King Phineus. When they had finished eating, the grateful King thanked them for the first meal he'd had for a long time. Then he said to Jason, "Go on your voyage, but beware of the Clashing Rocks. When a ship sails between them, they crash together, smashing the ship." And he told Jason how to deal with this danger.

Aboard The Argo again, the crew rowed away from the island, and next day, came to the entrance to the Black Sea. Ahead of them were towering cliffs on either side of a narrow channel. These were the Clashing Rocks. Jason flung a dove he had brought with him into the air. It flew straight between the Rocks which clashed together, just catching a few of the bird's tail feathers. When the Rocks parted again, Jason shouted, "Row for your lives," and the crew pulled with all their strength on the oars.

As the ship raced between the rocks, they began to move together again. But the goddess Athene saw the danger and sent a great wave which pushed the ship through the closing gap. The Rocks clashed together with a thunderous crash a second after The Argo had slid safely past. The crew rowed on, into the calm Black Sea.

The ship sailed on, calling at islands and ports; sometimes the Argonauts were welcomed and sometimes they had to fight to escape. At last, they reached the river which led to Colchis and moored for the night.

Fire-Breathing Bulls and Dragons' Teeth

Next morning, Jason and two friends set off for the magnificent palace of King Aeetes. He was a cruel king who ruled his land very harshly. He came out to meet them, welcoming them and pretending to be friendly. "I've come for the Golden Fleece," explained Jason. "When I take it back to Uncle Pelias, I can claim the throne."

"You may have the Fleece," said King Aeetes, who was quite determined not to let it go, "but first you will have to carry out the tasks that I give you." Jason said he would do anything King Aeetes asked.

"You must harness two fire-breathing bulls and drive them across a field. Then you must sow the field with dragons' teeth," ordered the King.

Standing near King Aeetes and listening to every word he said was his daughter, Medea. She had fallen in love with

Jason the moment she first saw him and decided to use her magic powers to help him. She knew he could never succeed on his own.

That night she crept out of the palace and picked herbs on the mountains. She made them into an ointment, chanting magic spells as she mixed it. She secretly gave this to Jason, telling him to rub it all over his body. It would protect him from the fire breathed by the bulls.

Next morning, Jason bravely strode out to the field to face the bulls. King Aeetes, Medea, the Argonauts, and all the people from the city came to watch. He walked to the bulls' cave and they came roaring out at him, bellowing, breathing fire, and stamping on the ground with their bronze hoofs.

The flames scorched the earth around Jason but didn't touch him. Medea's magic ointment worked well. Jason walked up to the huge bulls, leapt on the back of one of them, grabbing its horns. Then he forced both bulls to kneel down. Stroking them to quiet them, he slipped the harness over their heads.

The amazed crowd watched in silence as Jason drove the two bulls across the field, turning the earth. All day he worked, walking up and down the field until it was finished. King Aeetes, furious that Jason had succeeded so far, then handed him a helmet full of dragons' teeth.

Jason walked up and down the field again, planting the teeth. Where each one landed on the ground, a fully armed soldier sprang up in its place. Jason had been told by Medea what to do. He picked up a huge rock and hurled it into the middle of the soldiers. They thought they were being attacked and started to fight each other. Soon they all lay wounded or dead.

The people cheered and shouted, but King Aeetes was silent with anger and Medea turned away to hide her smiling face. She was afraid her father would suspect she had helped Jason.

The Golden Fleece

That night Medea crept out of the palace and ran down to the river where the Argonauts were sleeping on The Argo. "Jason," she whispered, shaking him to wake him up. "My father is planning to kill you all and burn your ship tonight. You must leave at once."

Jason woke the crew and silently they rowed The Argo away from the city and hid it in the reeds by the river bank.

"Come with me," said Medea, and she led Jason through the dark woods to a giant oak tree. Hanging from a branch was the Golden Fleece, but coiled around its trunk was the huge serpent with golden eyes which it never closed. When it saw Jason and Medea, it hissed and showed its fangs.

Medea walked up to it, singing a magic spell. The serpent slowly closed its eyes and was soon fast asleep. Jason quickly climbed up the tree, grabbed

the Golden Fleece from its branch, and slid down again. He and Medea raced through the woods, back to the ship. "I have the Golden Fleece," Jason shouted to the Argonauts. "We must leave at once."

Jason and Medea jumped on board The Argo, and the crew rowed as fast as they could down the river to the open sea. But one of the King's guards saw them and ran to the King with the news. King Aeetes was furious that Jason had the Golden Fleece, and ordered his fastest ships to sail after The Argo. "We must find him and get the Golden Fleece back," he shouted.

The King's fast ships chased The Argo and caught up with it. There were many battles before the Argonauts escaped and sailed home to Iolcus.

Jason took the Golden Fleece to Pelias and demanded the throne in return. Pelias was amazed and not pleased that Jason had returned safely, but had to agree.

Jason lived happily with Medea for many years. She inherited the throne of Corinth, and Jason became king there too, ruling both kingdoms wisely and well.

King Midas

King Midas was a foolish, greedy king but he could also be kind and generous. When Silenus, an old satyr who had the body of a goat and the head of a man, arrived at his palace, tired and hungry from wandering in the hills, Midas fed him well and looked after him.

Silenus was a companion of the god Dionysus, who was pleased with the way the King had treated the satyr. Dionysus went to Midas. "I will grant you one wish. You may have anything you like," he said. Midas thought for a while and then he had an idea. "I would like everything I touch to turn into gold," he said.

"That could be dangerous. Are you sure that's a wise choice?" asked Dionysus. "Yes, yes, that's what I want," replied Midas, excitedly. "Very well," said Dionysus, "your wish is granted," and he vanished.

Midas looked around him. Then he put out his hand and gently tapped a table. It turned into shining gold.

"This is wonderful," laughed Midas, "I shall be the richest man in the world." He dashed around his palace, touching chairs, walls, doors, floors, pillars and ornaments, sacks of corn and cloth; and everything turned into solid gold.

He shouted for his servants to bring him a feast. As soon as it was laid on the golden table, he touched the plates. Midas had always longed to eat from gold plates. But when he picked up his food, that too turned to gold. He realized that he could eat and drink nothing.

His young son ran into the room calling, "Father, what's happened to the palace?" Midas patted his son and, at once, he turned into a golden statue. "What have I done?" cried King Midas.

That night, alone and hungry, Midas prayed to Dionysus to save him before he starved to death. "I did warn you," said Dionysus, suddenly appearing. "Tomorrow, go and bathe in the river and this curse will be lifted. And let that be a lesson to you."

Next morning, Midas hurried to the river and dashed into the water. When he came out, he touched the bank and it remained just mud. "It's over," he sighed. When he went back to the palace, everything that was gold was normal again, and his young son came running to meet him.

Midas had learned not to be greedy, but he was still foolish. One day, the gods Apollo and Pan had a competition to see who could play the best music. Apollo played his lyre so well the birds stopped singing to listen. Then Pan played his pipes; a sad and mournful sound.

The judge immediately announced that Apollo was the winner, but King Midas, who had been listening, said very loudly, "I think Pan was the best."

Apollo was furious. "There must be something wrong with your ears," he shouted. "Perhaps they are too small. I'll make them bigger," and he pointed his finger at Midas.

The King put his hands on his head and felt two long furry ears, just like the ears of a donkey. Hiding his head under his cloak, he rushed away to the palace.

He didn't want anyone to see him and laugh at him. He put on a tall cap with the ears tucked inside. Every day he wore his cap and even kept it on in bed. But his hair grew longer and longer and, at last, he had to go to the barber.

Midas made the barber swear that he would never tell anyone about his ears. "If you so much as whisper it, you shall die," he said. The barber promised he would keep the secret. Weeks passed and the barber kept his promise, but he desperately wanted to tell someone.

When he could bear it no longer, the barber went to the river bank, dug a hole and whispered into it, "The King has donkey's ears." Then he filled in the hole and thought the secret would be safe.

In the spring, reeds grew up on the river bank. When the wind blew through them, they rustled and whispered, "The King has donkey's ears, the King has donkey's ears." Everyone now knew King Midas's secret and that he was a very foolish man.

The Adventures of Perseus

Blown by the wind, a huge wooden chest floated along on the sea and gently beached on the island of Seriphos. A fisherman found it, lifted the lid, and was astonished to see a woman and her baby son inside it.

They had been put there by the woman's father, King Acrisius, who had been told his grandson would kill him. Because he couldn't bear to kill his daughter, Danae, and his grandson, Perseus, he had them put in the chest and set it adrift on the sea.

The fisherman took Danae and Perseus to Polydectes, the king of the island, who was very kind and generous to them. Perseus grew up to be a clever and strong young man but he was unhappy because King Polydectes wanted to marry his mother, and he knew that, although Danae was grateful to the King, she always refused every time he asked her.

Polydectes decided that if Perseus was out of the way, Danae would change her mind. He called Perseus to him and said in a friendly voice, "Perseus, you have lived in my palace for long enough. It's time you proved what a brave and strong young man you are. I want you to bring me the head of Medusa, the Gorgon."

The Head of Medusa

Polydectes knew very well that many men had tried to kill Medusa, but failed. She was a hideous monster with snakes instead of hair, and anyone who looked at her was instantly turned to stone. He was sure that Perseus, too, would fail.

Perseus stared at Polydectes, and didn't feel very brave. But he knew he couldn't refuse the challenge. "I'll go at once," he said, "and I'll bring you Medusa's head."

The gods were watching Perseus and decided to help him. When he started his journey to Medusa, the goddess Athene appeared in front of him. "Take this shield," she ordered, and told him how to use it. The god Hermes gave him winged sandals so he could travel quickly, a helmet which made him invisible, a sickle, and a special bag.

With these gifts, Perseus flew far over the sea to the northern mountains where Medusa lived. At last, he landed on a rocky plain and followed a path to a cave. On each side were the statues of brave men who had looked at Medusa and been turned to stone. It was very quiet as Perseus strode along; even the animals and birds didn't go near this place.

When he reached the cave, Perseus did as Athene had told him, and looked at his shining shield, using it like a mirror. He could see Medusa in it. The monster was so hideous, he shivered with fright. She heard his footsteps, but couldn't see him because he was wearing the helmet that made him invisible. She crawled out of the cave, the snakes on her head hissing and spitting.

Keeping his eyes fixed on the shield, Perseus sprang forward. He raised the sickle and cut off Medusa's head. There was a terrible cry and Medusa lay dead.

Perseus picked up her head without looking directly at it for, even now, it could still turn him to stone. He opened his bag, stuffed the head in, and tied it up tightly with cord.

Andromeda

Slinging the bag over his shoulder, Perseus flew away from the land, over the sea to a distant southern shore. Looking down, he saw a beautiful girl chained to a rocky ledge. He swooped down like a bird and landed lightly at her side. "Who are you and what are you doing here?" he asked.

"My name is Andromeda," replied the girl, and she began to cry. Through her tears, she explained, "My mother, the queen, boasted that I'm more beautiful than the sea nymphs. The nymphs weren't very pleased about this, and complained to Poseidon, the god of the sea, who was so angry, he flooded my father's land. The only way my father could save his country was by sacrificing me to a sea monster which may come at any moment."

Perseus gazed at Andromeda, dazzled by her beauty, and then glanced over his shoulder at the sea. There, speeding through the waves, was a monster with huge eyes, a gaping mouth and a long, snake-like body.

Perseus soared up into the air and flew at the monster, slashing it with his sickle. The monster tried to grab Perseus with its fangs, but he dodged and dived in for another attack. Soon, the monster was wounded and lay writhing in the sea. With one final blow, Perseus killed it and it sank beneath the waves.

Perseus flew back to Andromeda and broke her chains to release her. Then he took her home to her father, King Cepheus. The King was so delighted that the monster was dead and his daughter was safe, he gave a great feast for Perseus. He also agreed that Perseus should marry Andromeda.

Together, they returned to Seriphos, where Perseus took Andromeda to meet his mother. She was overjoyed that Perseus had returned safely but looked very sad. "While you were away, King Polydectes forced me to agree to marry him," she said. "The wedding is tomorrow."

Very angry, Perseus rushed to the palace to confront the King. Polydectes was astonished and very frightened that Perseus had returned. "I've brought you Medusa's head," shouted Perseus. Careful not to look at it, he pulled it out of the bag, and held it up in front of the King. Instantly, Polydectes and all his friends were turned to stone.

Perseus gave the throne of Seriphos to the King's brother, who ruled the island happily and well. He gave the helmet, winged sandals, sickle and bag back to the gods, thanking them for their gifts. He married Andromeda and they were happy for many years.

The Prophecy

Perseus was a wonderful athlete who excelled at discus throwing, wrestling, running and throwing the javelin and spear. One year, the famous Greek games were held on his grandfather's island and Perseus decided to take part in them.

Many teams of athletes came to compete in the stadium, and everyone from the towns and villages on the island watched and cheered.

After the runners and wrestlers had competed, it was time for the discus throwers. Perseus walked to the stand, carrying his discus. Taking his position, he threw the discus as hard as he could. It flew through the air, but a gust of wind caught it and blew it off course. It hit King Acrisius on the head and he fell down dead. The prophecy had come true: King Acrisius was killed by his own grandson.

The Chariot of the Sun

At dawn every morning, the god Helios began his journey across the sky from the east. Driving his chariot of the sun, drawn by four horses, he brought light and warmth to the Earth. During the day, he saw everything that happened on the Earth. In the evening, his chariot sank down below the horizon in the west and it was dusk. During the night, Helios rode in a great golden bowl under the world to the east, ready to start his daily round again.

One day, Helios's son, Phaethon, went to his father. "Please, father," he begged, "will you grant me one wish?" Helios promised Phaethon he could have a wish. "I want you to let me drive your chariot, just for one day," said Phaethon. "My friends don't believe I'm your son, but if they saw me driving the sun across the sky, they would know you really are my father."

Helios didn't want his son to drive his chariot; his horses were very strong and wild, but he had promised and had to agree. "You must be careful," he said. "You must drive very steadily across the sky, not too high and not too low."

Next morning, Phaethon's sisters came to help him harness the horses. Laughing with excitement, Phaethon leapt into the chariot, shook the reins, and raced away. The horses soon sensed that the driver couldn't control them. They galloped up and up. The sun chariot was so high, it left a great scar of stars, the Milky Way, across the sky. Far below, the Earth began to freeze.

Terrified, Phaethon pulled and heaved on the reins with all his strength. The horses plunged down and down. Too close to the Earth, the sun scorched the ground, drying up the rivers, setting fire to the grass and trees, and making great deserts.

Zeus, the chief god, watched from his palace on Mount Olympus. "That foolish young man will destroy the world," he roared angrily. He pointed his fingers. At once, a thunderbolt shot from them and killed Phaethon. He fell down into a river and the sun chariot raced on to the west.

Phaethon's sisters stood on the bank of the river and wept for their dead brother. They cried so much, they turned into weeping willows which still stand, weeping, on river banks. Helios never, ever let anyone drive his sun chariot again.

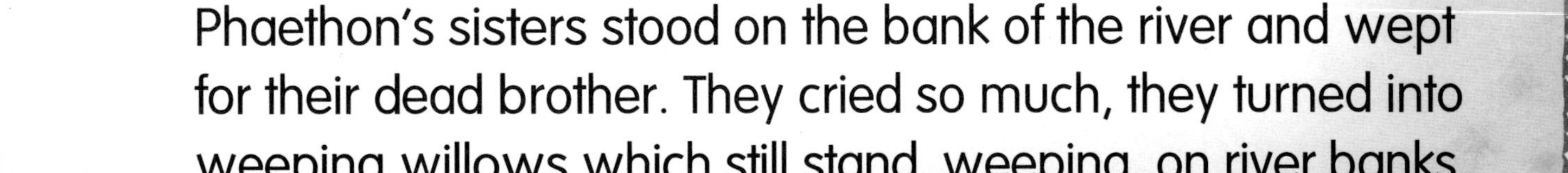

The Adventures of Odysseus

Odysseus sat slumped on the beach and stared out across the shimmering sea. In the nearby camp outside the city walls of Troy, he could hear his Greek soldiers grumbling. "It's no good. We can't win this war," growled one. "We've been here for ten years. Ten years! I vote we give up and go home," said another.

Odysseus groaned to himself. They're right, he thought. It's ten years since I left my beloved wife Penelope and little son Telemachus. Ten years since I left my island kingdom of Ithaca to fight in this war. All those years since Paris, the Trojan prince, captured Helen, who is said to be the most beautiful woman in the world, and took her to Troy. He groaned again.

Ten years ago, the Greeks, led by Odysseus, had gathered together an army and a great fleet of ships. Some said there were a thousand altogether. They had sailed to Troy to rescue Helen and bring her back to her husband, Menelaus. Although they had fought fierce battles with the Trojans and many had been killed, they could not break into the city of Troy.

Odysseus stood up and went in search of the other leaders. "The soldiers are getting restless. They want to go home," he said. "We can't give up now," replied one king. "I have an idea," said Odysseus, and he told them his plan.

The Wooden Horse

For many days, the Trojans watched from the tops of their city walls as the Greeks collected huge piles of wood on the beach. They sawed, cut and hammered it, while the Trojans wondered what the Greeks could be making.

Then, one morning, as the Trojan guards on the walls looked out at dawn, they were amazed to see that the beach was empty. The Greek camp and all the ships pulled up on the beach had vanished. Nothing was left but an enormous wooden horse. "They've gone. The war is over. We've won. We've won," the Trojans shouted. They opened the city gates and rushed down to the beach.

They stared at the wooden horse, walked all around it and tapped it. "Why have the Greeks left this?" one man asked. "It must be a gift for the goddess Athene," replied another. "We'll take it into the city."

The Trojans dragged the wooden horse into the city square. That evening, they all had a huge party, with masses of food and wine, to celebrate the end of the war. Then they sang and they danced until, at last, tired out, they went to bed.

When the whole city was quiet, the wooden horse creaked and a secret door opened. Inside were ten Greeks. "Don't make a sound," whispered Odysseus to his soldiers, and let down a rope. They slid down it, ran silently through the city, knocked out the sleepy guards, and opened the city gates.

In the night, the Greek fleet of ships had sailed back to Troy and the army was waiting on the beach. When the gates were opened, they rushed into the city. Before the Trojan men could get out of bed and grab their weapons, the Greeks killed them.

They rescued Helen, made the women and children their slaves, stole all the treasure and set fire to the city. Odysseus's plan had worked and the war was over. At last, they could go home, taking Helen with them. The Greeks divided the Trojan's treasure between them, loaded up their ships, and joyfully rowed away from the ruined city of Troy.

Odysseus and his men set sail and, in a great storm which lasted for days, became separated from the other ships. When the sea was calm again, they were alone.

They sailed on, stopping at islands where sometimes the crew had to fight battles to escape, and sometimes were welcomed and given food and water. Storms drove their ship across wild seas, and past rocky shores where they couldn't land. When the wind dropped, they had to row until they were too tired to go on.

Cyclops, the One-Eyed Giant

After many months, Odysseus and his men reached an island where they landed to find food and water. There were no people, but at the top of the cliff they could see a huge cave. "We'd better explore," said Odysseus. He picked up a skin full of wine and led his men across the island. As they found no one, they decided to climb the cliff to the cave.

Odysseus stopped at the entrance, peered in and shouted, "Anyone there?" There was no reply. He stepped in and looked around. In the cave were enormous bowls of milk and cheese. "Let's eat while we wait for the owners to come back," Odysseus said to his hungry men.

Suddenly, they heard a thunderous noise and sprang to their feet. A Cyclops, a giant with only one eye, filled the entrance, blocking out the sun. He herded a flock of sheep into the cave. Then he rolled a massive rock across the entrance to close it like a door.

The Cyclops glared at the Greeks with his one huge eye.

"Who are you and what are you doing in my cave?" he roared. "We are Greek soldiers on our way home to Ithaca from Troy," said Odysseus. "We were looking for fresh food and water."

Before they could move, the Cyclops grabbed two men in his enormous fist, and stuffed them into his mouth. Odysseus and his men stared in horror. "Quick, get behind those rocks," whispered Odysseus, and they dashed to a dark corner of the cave. They watched the Cyclops lie down and go to sleep.

"We must kill him before he eats us all," whispered one of the men. "No," replied Odysseus. "If we kill him, we'll be trapped in here. We'd never be able to move that rock from across the entrance. We must wait."

Next morning, the Cyclops woke up, rolled away the rock and herded his sheep out of the cave. Before Odysseus and his men could slip out, he rolled the rock back again, trapping them inside the cave. "I've a plan," said Odysseus. "I need a big wooden pole." They searched the cave until they found one, and hid it behind some rocks. Then they waited until the Cyclops came back.

In the evening, the Cyclops rolled back the rock and herded in his sheep, closing the entrance again. Odysseus poured wine from his wine skin into a huge bowl. He offered it to the Cyclops, who drank the wine, and Odysseus filled the bowl again.

"What's your name?" asked the Cyclops. "I'm called Nobody," said Odysseus, pouring more wine into the bowl. "That's a very strange name," laughed the Cyclops, and he lay down and was soon snoring loudly.

"Now's our chance," Odysseus said to his men. "Bring me the pole from behind the rocks." Holding the pole, Odysseus crept up to the sleeping Cyclops and pushed it into his one eye.

The Cyclops leapt up and stumbled around the cave, shouting and roaring. The other Cyclops on the island heard the noise. "What's the matter?" they called. "Nobody has hurt me. Nobody has blinded me," cried the Cyclops. "If nobody has hurt you, why are you making all that noise?" they asked and they went back to their caves, muttering, "He's gone crazy."

Next morning, the Cyclops rolled away the rock from the cave to let out his sheep.

"You'll never escape," he shouted, but Odysseus had a plan. He tied the sheep together in threes. "Lie down and hold onto a middle sheep," he ordered his men. As the sheep trotted past the Cyclops, he stroked their backs but he didn't feel the men clinging on underneath.

When they were all outside the cave, Odysseus shouted, "Run for the ship." They raced down to the shore and rowed their ship away as fast as they could. The Cyclops heard them go and roared with rage. He hurled huge rocks at the ship, but as he couldn't see it, they all missed. Odysseus and his men thought they were safe.

The Cyclops was the son of Poseidon, the god of the sea. He begged his father to take revenge on the Greeks who had blinded him. Poseidon promised he would punish them.

A Bag of Winds

Odysseus and his men sailed on and landed on another island. There King Aeolus, who was the keeper of the winds, welcomed them. He held feasts for them and they stayed happily for many weeks with the King, his wife and their sons and daughters.

When it was time to leave, King Aeolus gave Odysseus a leather bag. "I've put in it the north, south and east winds," he said, "but left out the west wind. This gentle wind will blow you eastward to Ithaca." Odysseus thanked the King and took the bag on board his ship.

As soon as the crew hoisted the sail, the west wind wafted the ship along. Odysseus didn't tell his men what was in the leather bag and they were curious. One day, when Odysseus was asleep, one man said, "Let's open the bag. Perhaps there's treasure in it," and he untied it.

Out flew the north, south and east winds in a terrible storm, which blew the ship back the way it had come. There was nothing they could do to stop it.

Circe's Magic

The ship raced on and, at last, reached another island. Odysseus sent a group of men, led by Eurylochus, to find food and water while he and the other men guarded the ship. He didn't want to be captured by more giants.

Eurylochus and his friends set off, and walked for hours without meeting anyone. At last, they saw a palace through the trees. When they reached it, a beautiful woman came out. She smiled at them. "I'm Circe. Come in. You must be hungry."

She led them into a huge hall where huge plates of food were laid out on a table. The men ate and drank as much as they could. They laughed and sang, thanked Circe for her kindness, and didn't even notice that Eurylochus wasn't with them. He had been suspicious of this woman; when the men had gone into the palace, he had stayed outside and watched through a window.

As soon as the feast was over, Circe waved her magic

wand and the men instantly turned into pigs. Then she drove them, grunting, out of the palace. Eurylochus ran back to the ship and told Odysseus what he had seen.

"I must rescue them," said Odysseus and, picking up his weapons, he ran to the palace. On the way, he was startled to see Hermes, the messenger of the gods, flying near him. "The goddess Athene sent me to give you this flower," called Hermes. "Eat it and you'll be safe from Circe's magic."

Odysseus thanked him and quickly ate the white flower. When he reached the palace, Circe came out to meet him. "Come in," she smiled. "You must be hungry." Odysseus thanked her and went in, certain he would be safe.

Circe handed him a cup of wine which had a magic potion in it. She watched Odysseus drink it and then tapped his arm with her magic wand. Instead of turning into a pig, Odysseus jumped up and pointed his sword at her. "Take me to my men," he ordered.

Circe was terrified because her magic hadn't worked. She led Odysseus out of the palace to a pen full of pigs. "Change them back," commanded Odysseus. Circe rubbed magic ointment over the pigs and, immediately, they became human again.

"Come back to my palace, and we will have another feast. No more magic potions, I promise you," said Circe. Odysseus and his men accepted. They sent for the men guarding the ship and stayed with Circe, enjoying themselves, for a whole year.

At last, Odysseus sighed and said, "It's time we went home." Circe was very sad. She had fallen in love with Odysseus, but knew he had to leave her. She gave him food and water for the voyage, and warned him of the many new dangers that were ahead of him.

The Sirens

Odysseus's ship sailed on and soon came to a very rocky island. Here Sirens, who were sea nymphs, sat on the rocks and sang enchanting songs to the ships that passed. Sailors were lured to the island, their ships were wrecked on the rocks and they were drowned. Circe had warned Odysseus about the Sirens, but he wanted to hear their songs.

"Tie me to the mast," he told his men, "and then fill your ears with beeswax. Don't take it out until we are well past this island." They did as he ordered. Then they started to row. The Sirens sang their enchanting songs but the men couldn't hear them. Furious that the ship was getting away, the Sirens sang louder and louder. Only Odysseus fell under their spell, and struggled with the ropes that held him.

"Untie me, let me free. They're calling me. I must go to them," he shouted, but the men couldn't hear him. They rowed steadily on and on until they were at a safe distance. Then they untied Odysseus's ropes and took the wax out of their ears.

Scylla and Charybdis

Odysseus and his men sailed on until, in front of them, they saw towering cliffs with a narrow channel between them. Then they heard a great roaring noise. In the channel was a giant whirlpool, a mass of swirling water which sucked ships down to the bottom of the sea. It was called Charybdis. They had to go through the channel. There was no other way.

Odysseus shouted, "Row as hard as you can. Pull for your lives." He steered the ship as close to the cliffs as he dared, so they could slip past the whirlpool. The men rowed hard, watching the whirlpool. They didn't see the Scylla, the six-headed monster, loom out of her cave high up on the cliffs. Suddenly, she shot out her six heads and snatched up six men. They shouted once, then were silent. She had swallowed them.

"Row on," shouted Odysseus. Soon the ship was out of reach of the Scylla and past the whirlpool. The wind blew, filling the big sail, and the tired crew could rest.

The Sacred Cattle

The ship soon reached another island. Odysseus warned his men not to touch the cows here. "They belong to the god Helios," he said. The men hunted wild animals and fish to eat but, when Odysseus was away from the camp, they killed and roasted a calf.

When Odysseus returned and found them eating meat, he was afraid. "The gods will punish us for this," he said. Helios found out what they'd done and was really angry.

Storm and Shipwreck

After a week on the island, Odysseus and his crew put to sea again. At first, the ship sailed gently along but then the wind grew stronger and stronger. Dark clouds filled the sky, and thunder crashed. The storm had been sent by Helios. "Take down the sail," shouted Odysseus. The crew struggled but it was too late. The mast snapped and fell over the side. Then a huge wave washed over the ship, turning it over and sinking it.

Odysseus clung to the broken mast, shouting again and again to his men, but they had all drowned. The wind and waves pushed the mast along until, after nine days, it washed up on a beautiful island.

The Goddess Calypso

The island was ruled by the goddess Calypso. She took Odysseus to her palace where he lived, enchanted by her, for seven years. She loved him and begged him to stay with her forever. But each day he sat on the beach, staring out to sea and longing for his rocky island of Ithaca.

At last, the goddess Athene went to Zeus and said, "It's time we helped this wanderer to go home." Zeus agreed and sent his messenger, Hermes, to tell Calypso she must let Odysseus go. Calypso had to obey the order and gave Odysseus the wood and tools he needed to build a boat.

When it was finished, Calypso sadly said goodbye to Odysseus. He sailed for days with a good breeze but then Poseidon, to avenge his son, the Cyclops, whom Odysseus had blinded, sent a terrible storm. It wrecked the small ship and flung Odysseus into the sea.

Athene wouldn't let Odysseus drown. She watched as he clung to the wreckage of his ship until he saw land. He swam to it and crawled, soaked and exhausted, up the beach, where he lay in despair.

Next morning, a princess was walking along the shore, and found Odysseus still lying on the beach. She took him to her father, King Alcinous, who greeted him kindly and fed and clothed him. When Odysseus told him of his voyage, the King said, "Your island of Ithaca is quite near here. Stay here tonight and tomorrow one of my ships will take you home."

Home at Last

At dawn, Odysseus boarded a ship, lay down and fell asleep. He was still fast asleep when the ship reached Ithaca. The sailors carried him ashore and left him on the beach. Then they sailed the ship away.

Poseidon, the god of the sea, was watching. He was angry that Odysseus had reached home safely and, to take revenge on the sailors who had helped him, he rose above the waves and pointed at the ship. In an instant, the ship turned to stone. Poseidon smiled and sank down into the sea again.

Odysseus woke up on the beach and looked around him. He didn't know where he was. Suddenly, a beautiful woman appeared. "I am the goddess Athene," she said. "I've come to help you. You've been away from Ithaca for so long, many people think you're dead and will never come back. The nobles on the island want to marry your wife, Penelope, and take your kingdom."

Odysseus leapt up. "I must go and save her," he said. "Not so fast," said Athene. "These men want to get rid of your son Telemachus, and they will kill you, too. But I have a plan. I'll disguise you as an old beggar. You are then to go to the swineherd's hut. I'll send Telemachus to meet you there." She raised her hand and Odysseus at once looked like an old beggar, dressed in rags.

He thanked Athene and hurried to the hut. The swineherd didn't recognize Odysseus. "Come in and eat with me," he said. "There's not much but you must be hungry." Odysseus thanked him and, after they had eaten, he said, "Tell me what's happening on Ithaca".

"Bad news," said the swineherd. "King Odysseus sailed for Troy twenty years ago and hasn't been heard of since." The door of the hut opened and a tall young man stepped in. "Prince Telemachus," cried the swineherd, jumping up.

"Who's this?" asked Telemachus, looking at Odysseus. Odysseus stood up. "I am your father," he said.

"You can't be. You're a beggar," cried Telemachus. "The goddess Athene disguised me so no one would recognize me," replied Odysseus. "Now, I've heard that the nobles want to marry your mother. Tell me about them."

Telemachus stared at Odysseus, wondering if what he

said was true. Then he said, "They come every day and ask my mother which one of them she will marry. She used to say she would choose one when she had finished her weaving. But then they found out that each night she unpicked her day's weaving so that it would never be finished. They're really unpleasant now. They eat and drink our food and wine, and I know they want to kill me."

Odysseus, Telemachus and the swineherd hurried to the palace. There the nobles were feasting as usual. Odysseus shambled in and begged for food. They all gave him a few scraps, except one who threw a stool at him.

After the nobles had gone to bed that night, Odysseus and Telemachus took all the weapons from the hall and hid them in the cellar. Penelope had heard there was a beggar in the hall and sent for him.

Odysseus kept his face in shadow; he didn't want Penelope to recognize him yet. "Have you heard any news of Odysseus?" asked Penelope. "He is alive and well, and will soon return to Ithaca," Odysseus growled to disguise his voice. "Thank you," sighed Penelope. "My old nurse will give you food." Odysseus quietly left the room.

The Test of Strength

When the nobles came into the hall the next morning, Odysseus was there waiting for them. He listened to them talking and grumbling about Penelope, but said nothing. After they had eaten breakfast, Penelope walked in, carrying a huge bow. "I have decided to give you all a test of strength," she said. "This bow belonged to my husband Odysseus. I will marry the man who can put the string on and shoot an arrow through the handles of twelve axes."

Telemachus set up the target of the twelve axes. The nobles argued about who should go first. They were all eager to show how strong they were. The first one picked up the bow and tried to put on the string, but however hard he struggled, he couldn't even bend the bow. The others jeered at him. Then they tried, one after the other, but they all failed. They grumbled that the bow was old and stiff; it wasn't that they weren't strong enough.

Odysseus stepped forward. "May I try?" he asked. The nobles jeered. "A beggar wants to marry a queen," sneered one. "Let him try," ordered Penelope. Odysseus whispered to Telemachus, "Take your mother to her room."

Telemachus hurried away with Penelope, and soon returned. Very quietly, he closed and locked the doors of the hall.

Odysseus picked up the bow, bent it easily, and put on the string. He slotted an arrow on the bow, pulled, and shot it straight through the twelve axes.

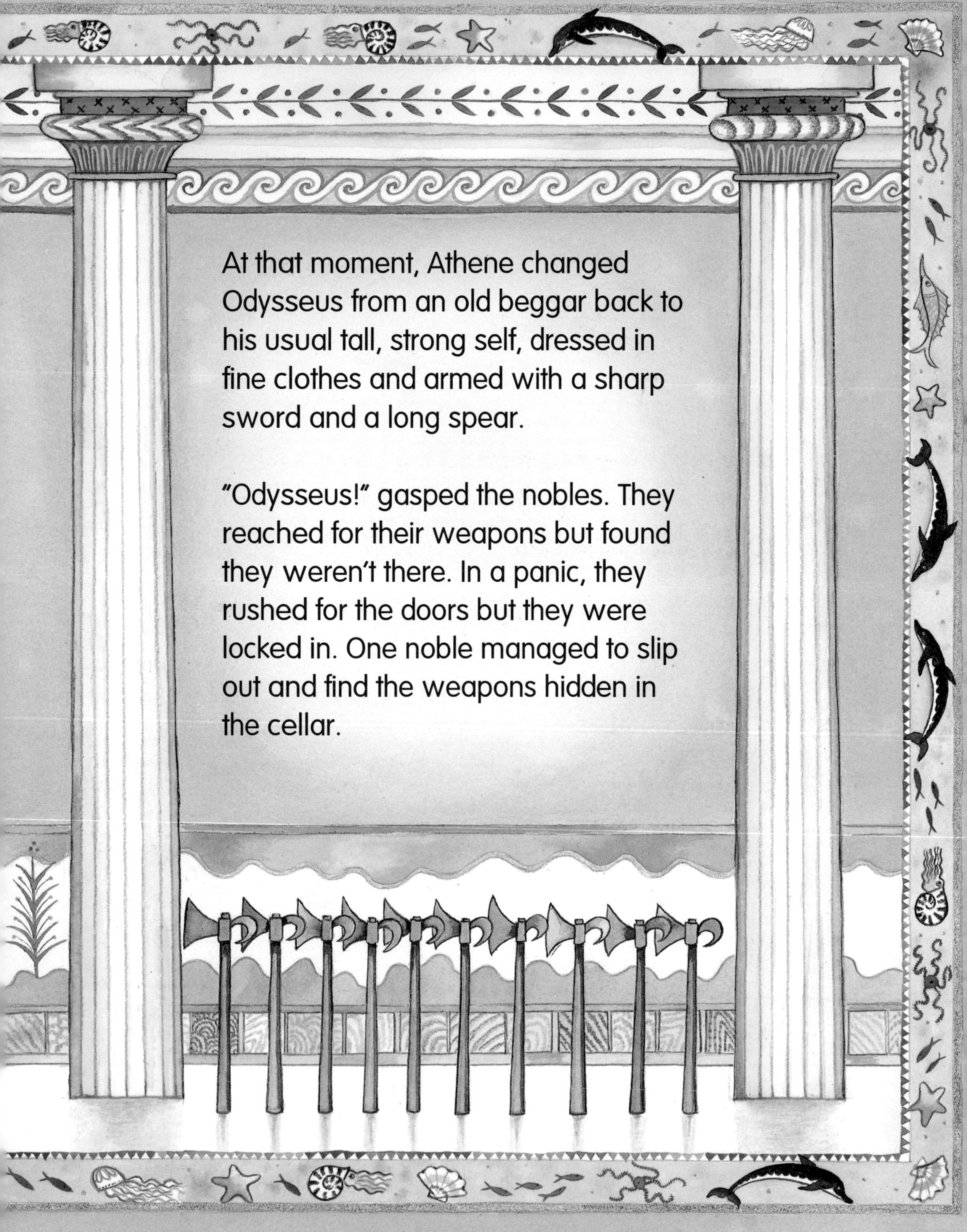

At that moment, Athene changed Odysseus from an old beggar back to his usual tall, strong self, dressed in fine clothes and armed with a sharp sword and a long spear.

"Odysseus!" gasped the nobles. They reached for their weapons but found they weren't there. In a panic, they rushed for the doors but they were locked in. One noble managed to slip out and find the weapons hidden in the cellar.

Drawing his sword, Telemachus ran to his father's side and together they fought a terrible battle. Although they were hugely outnumbered, they managed to kill all the nobles.

The old nurse, who was hiding behind a pillar, ran to tell Penelope what she had seen. Penelope hurried to the hall. She stared at Odysseus. She hadn't seen him for twenty years. "Are you really my husband or is this a trick the gods are playing on me?" she asked. "Yes, my dear and faithful wife," replied Odysseus, "I am."

Penelope was still not certain and thought of a test. "Go to my bedroom and move the bed into another room," she said to the old nurse. "You can't do that. I built that bed around a tree. It can't be moved," said Odysseus. "Only you and I know about the tree. That proves you are really Odysseus," said Penelope, and she threw her arms around him.

"Yes, I've come home at last to reclaim my wife, and my kingdom," replied Odysseus, smiling at her. "And you'll never believe all the adventures I have to tell you and my brave son Telemachus about."

Theseus and the Minotaur

The Minotaur was a terrible monster, which lived in a maze, called the Labyrinth, under the palace of King Minos of Crete. Half man and half bull, it ate humans. Because the son of King Minos had been killed in Athens, he demanded that, every year, seven girls and seven young men were sent from Athens to Crete to be fed to the Minotaur.

Theseus, the son of the King of Athens, was a very brave, clever young man who loved adventures and who could never resist a challenge. One year, he offered to sail to the island of Crete as one of the seven young men. He was determined to kill the Minotaur.

When the fourteen young Athenians reached Crete, they were taken to King Minos's palace. There the King's daughter, Ariadne, at once fell in love with Theseus; he was so good-looking. She went to him secretly when he was alone. "I'll help you kill the

Minotaur if you'll marry me," she whispered. Theseus looked at the lovely princess for a moment, and agreed.

Very early one morning, Ariadne led Theseus to the entrance of the Labyrinth. She tied one end of a ball of string to the door post and gave the ball to Theseus. "Take this and let it unwind as you go in," she said. "Then you will be able to follow the string when you come back. Without it, you'll never find your way out again." Theseus thanked her and bravely strode into the Labyrinth, letting out the string as he went.

He walked down long twisting tunnels and winding passages, around many corners, farther and farther into the maze. At last, he could hear the Minotaur bellowing and shaking the ground with its stamping hoofs.

His sandals making no sound on the stone floor, Theseus crept closer until, rounding the last corner, he saw the huge monster. It sensed him and raised its head, red eyes glaring.

Then it bellowed and charged. Dodging its massive horns, Theseus struck the Minotaur again and again with his sword. The monster bellowed again, almost deafening Theseus, but he fought on until, at last, the Minotaur sank to the ground and lay still. It was dead.

Pausing only to get his breath back, Theseus caught hold of the string and, winding it up as he went, he raced back through the twisting tunnels of the Labyrinth to the entrance where Ariadne was waiting for him. "I've killed the Minotaur," he gasped, "but we must hurry before your father finds out."

It was still early in the morning and the sleepy guards rubbed their eyes as Theseus and Ariadne ran through the palace to where the young Athenian girls and men were locked in their rooms.

Theseus quickly released them. "Go back to our ship but don't make a noise," he said quietly. They followed Theseus and Ariadne down to the shore where their ship was moored. Leaping on board, the sailors rowed away from Crete and out to sea where, hoisting the sail, they sped over the water safely back to Athens.

Pygmalion and His Wife

Pygmalion sighed as he chipped away at a huge block of pure white marble in his workshop. He was a very clever sculptor who made beautiful statues, but he was sad and lonely because he couldn't find a wife.

An old friend watched him working. "Cheer up. There are lots of lovely girls you could marry," he said. "That's not true," said Pygmalion, sighing again. "I've met many of them but I can't fall in love with any one of them. Some of them are very pretty but they're all cold and hard-hearted. And look at all the unhappy marriages. So many of the wives behave very badly to their husbands. I don't want that sort of wife."

Pygmalion spent many weeks working on his latest statue. It was the best he had ever made. When it was finished, it was of a very beautiful girl, and the more Pygmalion gazed at her, the more he fell hopelessly in love with her. He hung a garland of flowers around her neck, and kissed her cold marble cheek.

A few days later, there was a special festival for Aphrodite, the goddess of love. Pygmalion went to her temple with an offering. For hours, he knelt in front of her statue and prayed, begging her to make the lovely statue in his workshop come alive.

At last, he went home, sad and tired, and fell asleep. But Aphrodite had heard Pygmalion's prayers and felt sorry for this unhappy man. She decided to help him.

Next morning, Pygmalion walked into his workshop and gazed at the statue. Somehow she seemed different. He rubbed his sleepy eyes and looked again. Then he touched her cheek. It wasn't cold marble but warm and soft human flesh. The staring eyes were now bright, and the stiff body moved a little. The statue had come alive.

Filled with joy, Pygmalion fell on his knees and thanked Aphrodite. He soon married his lovely, living statue. He called her Galatea and they were very happy together.

Eros and Psyche

"My daughter is the most beautiful girl in the world," boasted Psyche's father. "She is even more beautiful than Aphrodite," added her mother. Aphrodite, the goddess of love, overheard them boasting, and was absolutely furious. How could any ordinary mortal girl be more beautiful than a goddess? She stormed off to find her son, Eros.

Eros was a mischievous youth who had a bow and magic arrows. When he shot someone with one of these arrows, they felt no pain but they fell instantly in love with anyone they saw.

"Eros," commanded Aphrodite, "I want you to make that wretched girl Psyche fall in love, preferably with a hideous monster."

Eros at once went in search of Psyche. He enjoyed making the most unlikely people, even the gods, fall in love. He found Psyche asleep on a grassy mountain slope. He pulled out an arrow from his quiver, but stumbled on a stone and the arrow went straight into his own leg. He immediately fell deeply in love with Psyche.

He gazed at Psyche, wondering what to do. If Aphrodite ever found out he loved this beautiful girl, she would be furious with him. Somehow he had to keep it a secret. After a while, Eros thought of a plan. He carried Psyche, who was still asleep, to his wonderful palace and laid her gently on a bed. Then he left her.

That night, and for many nights, Eros went to the palace when it was dark and left each morning before it grew light at dawn. At first, Psyche was frightened by this man she was never able to see. But he was so gentle with her and spoke to her so sweetly, she soon looked forward to his visits. "You must never try to find out who I am," he warned her.

Psyche's sisters heard she was living alone in a fine palace and went to visit her. They wanted to know all about the mysterious man, and teased her. "Perhaps he already has a wife and lots of children," said one.

"Perhaps he won't let you see him because he's so hideous," laughed another. "Perhaps he's a monster," giggled a third sister.

"Go away. I won't listen to you," Psyche said, putting her hands over her ears. But when her sisters had gone, she felt just as curious as they did. She longed to see him.

That night, when Eros was asleep, Psyche crept downstairs and lit a tiny oil lamp. She tiptoed back with it and held it up so she could look at the man she had never seen before. She was overjoyed that he was young and so handsome, and knew she loved him.

Leaning over him for a closer look, a drop of hot oil from the lamp fell on his arm. He woke up and glared angrily at Psyche. Then he leapt up and, without saying a word, he stormed out of the palace into the dark night.

Psyche threw herself down on the bed and cried until the dawn. All day she wandered sadly through the palace and, that night, waited, hoping desperately that the man she had seen would come to her. But, although she lay awake all night, he never came.

For weeks, Psyche waited and wept. Then for months she searched everywhere for the man she loved. When she could bear it no longer, she prayed to Aphrodite. "Goddess of love, please help me," she begged.

Aphrodite heard her but wouldn't easily forgive her. "It's my son Eros you love, but you can't expect a god to love a silly mortal girl like you," she said. "Though he just might come back to you, if you do the tasks I give you." Psyche promised she would do anything.

Aphrodite took her to a barn. On the floor was a huge pile of corn, rye and barley. "Your first task is to separate this grain into three different heaps by the end of the day," said Aphrodite.

Psyche sat down and began to sort the grain. After an hour or so, she realized it would take her years to finish the task.

She stared at the huge pile of grain in despair. Then she saw a long column of ants marching across the floor. When they reached the pile, each ant picked up a grain and carried it to one of the three heaps. By evening, all the grain had been sorted into heaps of corn, rye and barley. Then the ants marched away.

Aphrodite was not pleased that Psyche had completed the task. She didn't know that Eros had sent the ants to help Psyche. "Your next task is to fetch a box of Persephone's beauty ointment from the Underworld," she said.

Poor Psyche didn't even know how to find the entrance to the Underworld. But with more secret help from Eros, she bravely went in, crossed the River Styx with the boatman, and came to the throne of Persephone. The Queen of the Underworld gave Psyche the box of ointment and, with Eros's help, Psyche quickly found her way out of the Underworld again.

She had been warned that she must not open the box. But Psyche thought if she just put a little beauty ointment on her face, she would be more beautiful and Eros might love her again. Stopping for a moment, she lifted the lid of the box. It didn't have beauty ointment in it but everlasting sleep which was death. At once, Psyche fell asleep.

Eros, who was watching, rushed to Psyche, and blew the sleep out of her eyes to wake her up. Psyche then took the box to Aphrodite while Eros flew to Zeus, the most powerful of all the gods.

"Please, Zeus," begged Eros, "I want to marry Psyche, but I can't unless you first make her immortal." Zeus, who was in a good mood, smiled and agreed.

Eros took Psyche to Mount Olympus where he married her and they were very happy.

Greek Names

This is how to say the Greek names in this book. The parts of the words in **bold** letters are stressed.

Acrisius - a-**kriss**-ee-us
Aeetes - aye-**ee**-teez
Aeolus - ee-**ole**-us
Alcinous - al-**sin**-o-us
Andromeda - an-**drom**-med-a
Aphrodite - aff-ro-**die**-tee
Arachne - a-**rack**-nee
Ariadne - a-ree-**add**-nee
Artemis - are-**tem**-iss
Athene - a-**thee**-nee
Augean - awe-**gee**-an
Bellerophon - bell-**air**-oh-fon
Cepheus - see-**fee**-us
Cerebus - **ser**-ber-uss
Charon - **ka**-ron
Charybdis - ka-**rib**-dis
Cheiron - **khee**-ron
Chimaera - **kim**-ear-a
Circe - **sir**-see
Colchis - **kol**-chiss
Cyclops - **sye**-clops
Daedalus - **deed**-a-lus
Danae - **dan**-ee
Demeter - dee-**meet**-er
Diomedes - die-om-**ee**-deez
Dionysus - **die**-on-eye-sus
Epimetheus - epp-ee-**mee**-thyoos
Eurolochus - yoo-**ril**-o-kus
Eurystheus - you-**riss**-thyoos
Geryon - gair-**eye**-on
Helios - **hee**-lee-oss
Heracles - **hair**-a-kleez
Hermes - **her**-meez
Hesperides - hess-**pair**-ee-deez
Hippolyta - hip-**pol**-ee-ta
Iobates - eye-oh-**bar**-teez
Iolaus - ee-oh-**lay**-us
Iolcus - ee-**ol**-cuss
Knossos - **noss**-oss
Labyrinth - **lab**-er-inth
Lycia - lie-**see**-a
Medea - med-**ee**-a
Medusa - med-**yoos**-a
Midas - **my**-dass
Minos - **my**-noss
Minotaur - **my**-no-tor
Odysseus - oh-**dee**-see-us
Orpheus - or-**fee**-us
Pelias - **pee**-lee-ass
Persephone - per-**seff**-on-ee
Perseus - **per**-see-us
Phaethon - **feeth**-on
Phineus - **fin**-ee-us
Polydectes - pol-ee-**deck**-teez
Poseidon - poss-**eye**-don
Prometheus - prom-**ee**-thyoos
Psyche - **sye**-kee
Scylla - **sill**-a
Seriphos - **sair**-i-foss
Silenus - **sye**-lee-us
Stymphalian - stim-**fail**-ee-on
Telemachus - tell-ee-**mack**-us
Theseus - **thee**-syoos
Tiryns - **tie**-reens